SNOW WAR

Look for these
and other books
in
The Kids in Ms. Colman's Class series

#1 Teacher's Pet
#2 Author Day
#3 Class Play
#4 Second Grade Baby
#5 Snow War
#6 Twin Trouble

Jannie, Bobby, Tammy, Sara
Ian, Leslie, Hank, Terri
Nancy, Omar, Audrey, Chris, Ms. Colman
Karen, Hannie, Ricky, Natalie

THE KIDS IN MS. COLMAN'S CLASS

SNOW WAR

Ann M. Martin

Illustrations by Charles Tang

A
LITTLE APPLE
PAPERBACK

SCHOLASTIC INC.
New York Toronto London Auckland Sydney

No part of this publication may be reproduced in whole or in part, or stored in a retrieval system, or transmitted in any form or by any means, electronic, mechanical, photocopying, recording, or otherwise, without written permission of the publisher. For information regarding permission, write to Scholastic Inc., 555 Broadway, New York, NY 10012.

ISBN 0-590-69201-1

12 11 10 9 8 7 6 5 4 3 2 1   7 8 9/9 0 1 2/0

Printed in the U.S.A.   40

First Scholastic printing, January 1997

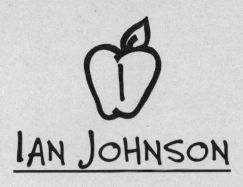

Ian Johnson

Ian Johnson was sitting in a cave. He was very happy. He was drinking cocoa and eating a chocolate-chip cookie. And he was reading *They Came from Beyond*. It was a space story that Ian had gotten for Christmas.

Ian had made the cave himself. He had made it by draping a blanket over the backs of two chairs. The blanket was big and heavy and dark, so there was not much light in Ian's cave. Ian was reading by flashlight. Also, Ian was hiding.

Ian was hiding from Chip. Chip was his fourteen-year-old brother, and he thought he knew everything. He especially

thought he knew way more than Ian did. Ian was tired of being teased by Chip. He hoped the new baby would be a girl.

Ian's mother was going to have a baby in three months. And then, thought Ian, I will be smack in the middle. At least *I* will not be the baby anymore. And at least Chip will have someone else to tease. Little Duncan or little Julia. (Those were the names Ian's parents had chosen for the baby.) But Ian was not sure he wanted a baby at all. He liked his family the way it was, even if Chip did tease him.

Ian turned another page in *They Came from Beyond*. The story was about creatures from a planet in another galaxy. The galaxy of Xantar. The planet was called X, and the creatures were called X-ers. This was the only thing Ian did not like about the book. If he had written the book himself, he would have come up with much more interesting names than X and X-ers. Maybe the planet Seldak, with creatures called Seldites. Anything was better than X and X-ers.

Still, Ian was enjoying the book very much. It was one of six science-fiction books his parents had given him for Christmas. Ever since Christmas, Ian had been reading and reading and reading. Now it was Sunday, the last day of vacation. On Monday, Ian would return to school. Ian liked school okay. And he liked his second-grade teacher, Ms. Colman, very much. But Ian was not ready to go back to school. All he wanted to do was read, and maybe play in the snow.

"Hey, Ian!" yelled Chip from downstairs.

"Yeah?"

"Chris is here. He wants you to come outside."

"Okay!"

Chris Lamar was one of Ian's good friends. He was in Ms. Colman's class too. Chris and Ian had gone sledding every day since Christmas. A lot of snow had been falling lately.

Ian ran downstairs. He was sorry to leave his tent and his book. But he did want to play with Chris on the last day of vacation. Playing on vacation is always more fun than playing on a regular day, thought Ian.

"Hi, Chris!" called Ian.

"Hi!" Chris replied.

Ian began to put on his snow pants and jacket and boots and mittens and hat.

(Getting dressed during the winter took forever.)

"Did you hear?" Chris asked while he waited.

"Hear what?" replied Ian.

"More snow tonight."

"Really? More snow? Cool. Maybe we will have a snow day tomorrow," said Ian. "Hey!" he cried. "A loose tooth!"

Ian put his finger on one of his front teeth. The tooth wiggled. Ian grinned. A snow day and a loose tooth. Not a bad way to end vacation.

2

SNOW

After dinner Ian listened to his new clock-radio. He listened to it all evening. Ian had tuned the radio to the local station. He wanted to hear storm coverage. (That was what Dr. G., the weatherman, called the weather report whenever a storm was on the way.) First Dr. G. said six inches were expected, then three, then just one. Ian hoped for six inches anyway. That might be enough to close school.

Ian was still very hopeful when he went to bed that night.

"Good night!" he called cheerfully to his family.

"Night, squirt," replied Chip.

Ian paid no attention to Chip. He lay in his bed, wiggled his tooth with his tongue, and planned to spend the next day reading in his tent. (And maybe sledding with Chris.)

As soon as his alarm went off in the morning, Ian jumped out of bed. He pulled up the window shade.

Not a flake of snow had fallen.

The road was clear, and two cars were whizzing by on it.

"Rats and toads," muttered Ian.

Ian listened to the radio while he got dressed — just in case. But of course Dr. G. did not say a thing about any schools being closed.

After breakfast Ian picked up his lunch and *They Came from Beyond*. He put his lunch in his backpack. Then he walked out the door reading his book. He read all the way to school. He read as he walked through the door to Stoneybrook Academy,

and while he walked along the hall to room 2A. In his classroom he stopped reading long enough to hang his coat in his cubby. Then he sat at his desk and read.

"Ian!" called Chris. "Come here!"

Chris was standing in a corner in the back of the room with Omar Harris, Bobby Gianelli, and Ricky Torres. They were looking at something Bobby was hiding in a paper bag.

"Later," said Ian.

Ian poked his nose back in his book. He was reading about the X-ers' plans to travel to the fourth planet from their sun. He did not look up for a long time. He did not look up when Tammy and Terri Barkan came into the room. Tammy and Terri were identical twins. He did not look up when Hank Reubens came in. Hank was another friend of Ian's. He did not look up when Karen Brewer, Hannie Papadakis, and Nancy Dawes came in. Karen, Hannie, and Nancy were best friends. They called themselves the Three Musketeers.

The Three Musketeers stood in the other back corner of the room. They looked at Chris, Omar, Bobby, and Ricky. Then they looked at each other and began to giggle.

Ian kept on reading. He read while Jannie Gilbert and Leslie Morris arrived. Jannie and Leslie were best friends. But they were the Three Musketeers' best enemies.

The X-ers were climbing into their spaceship when Natalie Springer, Audrey Green, and Sara Ford showed up. The X-ers were just about to blast off when Ian heard someone say, "Good morning, class! And welcome back. I hope you had a nice vacation."

Ms. Colman had arrived.

Her students scrambled for their seats. Ian turned around. He looked at the Three Musketeers in the row behind him, with Ricky. They were still giggling. Then he looked over at Chris. Chris had returned glumly to his seat.

That was how Ian felt. Glum. He frowned. He put *They Came from Beyond* in his desk. He would have to wait until recess to read it again.

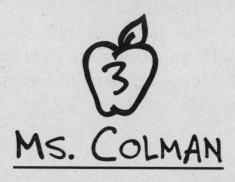

Ms. Colman

The sixteen kids in Ms. Colman's class sat quietly at their desks. They looked at their teacher.

"Hello, girls and boys," said Ms. Colman.

"Hi," replied the kids.

Ms. Colman smiled. "I wish we were still on vacation, too," she said.

Ian began to feel a bit better. He remembered why Ms. Colman was his favorite teacher. It was because she said things like that — that she wished she were still on vacation, too. Ms. Colman was honest, thought Ian. She understood kids. Plus, she made school (pretty much) fun. And she hardly ever yelled or got mad.

Ms. Colman took attendance. She asked the kids about their holidays. And then she said, "Class, I have an announcement."

Ms. Colman was smiling again, so Ian knew it would be a good announcement. He decided he felt even better.

"Since you are feeling sad about vacation," Ms. Colman began, "I will give you something to look forward to. At the end of January, Stoneybrook Academy will hold its winter carnival."

"The winter carnival!" exclaimed Jannie.

"Cool!" said Omar.

"What is the winter carnival?" asked Sara. (Sara was new to Stoneybrook Academy.)

Ian shot his hand into the air. "Can I tell her, Ms. Colman? Please?" he cried.

"Of course," said Ms. Colman.

"The winter carnival is the most fun

carnival ever," said Ian. "We have it at school every year. You can play games and win prizes. You can buy cookies and hot chocolate. And sometimes they have a raffle and you can win a bicycle or something."

"Wow," said Sara.

"The money that is made at the carnival," added Ms. Colman, "is used to buy new books for our library and classrooms, new equipment for our gym, and things like that."

"And every class has its own booth at the carnival. Right, Ms. Colman?" called out Karen.

"That's right," replied Ms. Colman.

"Last year when I was in first grade," said Hank, "our class had a booth called Go Fish. You could fish for prizes with real fishing rods. I caught a deck of cards."

"Once I played a ring-toss game and I won a whole set of markers," added Natalie.

"What will our booth be this year, Ms. Colman?" asked Sara.

"We will have a fortune-telling booth," said Ms. Colman. "A *winter* fortune-telling booth. We are going to cut out lots and lots of paper snowflakes. On most of the snowflakes we will write silly fortunes. But on a few of the snowflakes we will write 'prize.' We will sell the snowflakes for fifty cents. People will buy them to find out their fortunes. But if they happen to buy a prize snowflake, they will win a prize instead."

Ian was grinning. This sounded like fun.

"We are going to be very busy this month, class," Ms. Colman went on. "We must cut out hundreds of snowflakes. We must write the fortunes. We must choose the prizes. And we need to make our booth."

Ian looked around at his happy classmates. For the moment, he had forgotten about the X-ers.

4

RECESS

By lunchtime Ian was thinking about the X-ers again. He just had to know if they were going to be able to blast off. And if they would reach the fourth planet from their sun. So he stuck *They Came from Beyond* into his pocket before he left for the cafeteria.

At lunch Chris said, "Ian, sit here!"

Ian carried his tray to the table where the boys in his class were sitting. There were only six boys in Ms. Colman's class. Six boys and ten girls. This was not fair, thought Ian. He wished it were the other way around. Ten boys and six girls. But it was not. So the boys stuck together.

"Want to see what we were looking at in the paper bag this morning?" Chris asked Ian.

Ian did. But even more, he wanted to find out how the X-ers were doing. He did not want to be rude, though. So he said, "Sure."

Bobby pulled out the bag. "Go ahead. Look inside," he said. "But do not take it out."

Ian looked inside. "Cool! An ant farm!" he said softly.

"It is a miniature one," said Bobby. "I got it for Christmas. But we cannot let Ms. Colman see it."

"No," agreed Ian. "That would not be a good idea."

When the boys had finished their lunches, Omar jumped up. "Okay! Let's go outside now!" he said.

"Yeah, let's throw snowballs," said Ricky.

"Are the ants coming outside?" asked Ian.

"Hmm," said Bobby. "I do not want them to get cold."

"I will keep them warm for you," offered Ian. "I could put the bag under my coat. Then I could just, you know, read or something. So I would not bother the ants."

"Really?" said Bobby. "Okay. Cool."

Yes! thought Ian. He took the paper bag and carefully zipped it inside his coat. Then he went outside. He headed for a big rock under a tree at the edge of the playground. Just as he had hoped, there was no snow on the rock. It had melted away. And the rock was warm from the sun. Ian hopped onto the rock. He leaned against the tree. For a moment he looked out at the playground — at the swings and monkey bars and slides, at the playing field, which was now covered with snow, and at the hill that sloped gently into the far end of the playground.

Then with a happy sigh he pulled out *They Came from Beyond*. He began to read.

The rest of the kids in Ms. Colman's class played in the snow. They built snowmen and snowwomen and snowcats and snowdogs. They even built a snowteacher.

"Ian, come help us!" yelled Hank.

"I can't," Ian called back. "I have to keep the ants warm."

"Oh, yeah," said Hank.

But Ian heard Ricky say, "He just wants to read. That is all he does now. Read."

"He is a brain," added Leslie.

"Hey, Brain! Don't you want to build a snowfort?" called Hank. "Put the ants in your pocket."

"No thanks!" called Ian.

Ian's classmates all decided to build snowforts. They began three of them. By the time recess ended, the forts had just been started. But Ian could tell they were going to be very wonderful.

5

HURTLING THROUGH SPACE

That evening snow began to fall. Ian went to his room after supper. He looked out his window and watched the snow in the light of a street lamp. He tried not to feel too excited.

Ian lay on his bed. He wiggled his loose tooth with his tongue. He read *They Came from Beyond*.

"Ian!" called his father. "Are you doing your homework?"

"Um . . . yes," said Ian.

Ian stuffed the book under his pillow. Then he found his spelling list. He studied it. When he thought he knew how to spell every word on it, he put it away. He took out his book again. The X-ers were now hurtling through space.

Hurtling through space, Ian said to himself. Hmm. What does that mean?

Ian carried the book across the hall to Chip's room. "Chip?" he said. "What does 'hurtling through space' mean?"

Chip grinned. "It means barfing. Barfing while you travel. Oh, no. Wait. That would be *hurling* through space."

"Very funny," said Ian. He took the book downstairs. "Mom, what does 'hurtling through space' mean?" he asked.

"Well, it means speeding through space," she said. "Rushing through. Going so fast it would be hard to stop."

"Oh. Cool," said Ian. "Thanks."

Ian wished he could hurtle through space himself.

The last thing Ian did before he fell asleep was look out his window. The snow was still falling. Ian crossed his fingers.

The first thing Ian did when he woke up the next morning was look out his window. The snow had stopped falling. Two or three inches were on the ground.

Ian turned on his radio.

Not one single school was closed.

"Oh, barf," said Ian.

Ian walked into his classroom that day reading *They Came from Beyond*.

"Hi, Brain!" called the kids.

Ian did not mind. And when it was time for recess, he headed straight for the rock, even though he did not have an ant farm that needed to be kept warm.

While Ian read about the X-ers, the rest of the kids worked on the snowforts they had begun the day before. The boys — Bobby, Chris, Omar, Ricky, and Hank — worked on one. Karen, Hannie, Nancy, Sara, and Natalie worked on another. Leslie, Jannie, Audrey, Tammy, and Terri worked on the third.

Every now and then Ian looked up from his book and admired the forts. The boys' fort looked a little like an igloo. It curved upward. But they could not figure out how to keep the top on. The fort that Karen and her friends were building looked like a castle. The fort the other girls were building looked like a tiny house. The girls had even made windows in it, and carved out a doorway.

"Excellent fort," Ian said to Chris as he walked by the igloo later.

Recess was ending. The kids would have to wait until Wednesday to work on their forts again.

"Thanks, Brain," replied Chris. "Don't you want to help us with it?"

Ian shook his head. "Not while the X-ers are still hurtling through space."

"What?"

"Never mind. Come on. I'll race you to the door."

6

SNOWFLAKES

"Okay, class. Settle down," said Ms. Colman as Ian and his classmates ran into the room. "It is time to start working on our snowflake project."

"Let's put sparkles on the snowflakes!" Karen called from the back of the room. (She did not remember to raise her hand.)

"Indoor voice, Karen," Ms. Colman reminded her. "And please raise your hand next time." She paused. "Sparkles are a nice idea," she added.

"No, they are not," Ian heard someone whisper crossly.

"But there is something we need to

do," Ms. Colman was saying, "before we start making the snowflakes."

"We need to tell Bobby how stupid his stupid fort is," whispered Sara Ford. "Ours is much better."

Sara was sitting on one side of Ian. Omar was sitting on the other side. "No we do not," hissed Omar. "We need to kick in your stupid snowf — "

"Class," said Ms. Colman loudly. "Listen up. Please pay attention. This is im-

portant. Each class has been given forty dollars to spend on its project. That is our budget."

Ian looked around at his classmates. Why were they so crabby? This was supposed to be a fun project.

"What do you think we will need to spend our money on?" Ms. Colman asked her class.

"Paper?" suggested Jannie.

"Sparkles?" said Karen.

"We will probably need to spend a little money on supplies," agreed Ms. Colman, "but we already have most of the things we need here at school. What else?"

Ian raised his hand. "I know!" he said. "We have to buy the prizes."

"Right," said Ms. Colman. "How many?"

The kids thought.

Hannie said, "We could buy eight prizes that cost five dollars each. Or we could get ten that cost, um, four dol — "

"No, dope. *Five* dollars," muttered Leslie.

"No. It is four. Dumbhead," whispered Karen.

Ms. Colman did not hear the girls. A good thing, thought Ian. She would not like the way they were talking to each other.

In the end, Ms. Colman and her class decided to buy ten four-dollar prizes. Then Ms. Colman passed out paper and scissors. The kids cut out the first of their snowflakes.

SNOWBALLS

The X-ers had been traveling through space for weeks and weeks. They were traveling in their meteor-powered ship, the *Planet Jumper*. And they were supposed to reach the fourth planet from their sun in . . . thirty-one weeks.

"Thirty-one more weeks," said Ian to himself.

"What?" said Hank.

"Oh. Oh, nothing." Ian hid his book in the pocket of his jacket. Then he took a bite out of his sandwich. He had not realized he had been talking out loud.

"Come help us with our fort after lunch, Ian," said Omar. "Please?"

"We need you," said Bobby.

"Yeah. The girls have *two* forts," added Chris. "Karen and Sara and Nancy and Natalie and Hannie have one."

"And Leslie and Audrey and Jannie and the twins have another," said Omar. "And the one they are working on is . . . well . . ."

"It is *good*," said Ricky. "Admit it. So is the other one."

"Yeah. It is good," Chris agreed glumly. "And they brag about it all the time."

"Well, yours is good, too," said Ian. "I saw it. I have seen all three of them. But I just want to read."

Chris sighed. "Okay," he said.

The boys finished their lunches. "Come on!" cried Omar.

Omar, Chris, Bobby, Hank, and Ricky clattered out of the cafeteria. The girls were already outside. Ian followed slowly. His hand was on the book in his pocket. He could not wait to open it again.

Ian trotted across the playground. A snowball whizzed by his head. "Hey!" he yelled. He turned around.

Ian saw Leslie packing a snowball. She ran into her fort and flung it out at the boys' fort. The snowball smashed against the side. It made a dent in it.

Now it was Bobby's turn to yell. "Hey! Hey, Leslie! It took me a long time to build that!" Bobby packed up a snowball. He flung it at Leslie's fort. It missed and hit the other one.

"Thanks a lot, Leslie!" shouted Karen. "That was *your* fault." Karen threw a snowball at Leslie.

The fight was on.

"Oh, boy," said Ian. He hurried to his rock. He opened his book to Chapter Seven. He tried to forget about the snowballs.

The next day, Thursday, Ian ran to the rock as soon as he finished his lunch. He wanted to get to it before his classmates

started throwing snowballs again.

He just made it. The moment Ian sat on the rock, he heard an angry shout behind him.

"You stay *out* of our *fort*," Sara yelled at Jannie.

"You stay out of *ours*!" Jannie yelled back.

"We would not want to be in your stinky fort anyway!" Nancy shouted to Jannie. "Or in *yours*," she yelled to the boys.

Whoosh.

A snowball shot out of the boys' fort. It hit Natalie on the arm.

"Ow!" cried Natalie. She threw a snowball at Ricky. Then she threw one at Audrey.

Snowballs flew through the air. Ian watched for a moment. Then he returned to his book. While he read, he wiggled his tooth. Back and forth, back and forth. He hoped it would fall out soon.

When the bell rang, Ian snapped the

book shut. He ran across the playground. He ran by his friends. He noticed that when they lined up to go inside, they stuck with their groups. And the groups were not talking to one another.

THE SNOW WAR

The next day was Friday. Ian was glad. The week was almost over. On Saturday and Sunday he could read as much as he liked. And he would not have to listen to snowball fights.

On the playground that day, Ian kept looking up from the X-ers' adventures. He watched the three groups of kids. He watched Tammy sneak into the boys' fort and kick down part of a wall. He watched Chris run to Karen's fort and sit on it. Chris sat on the secret tunnel, and the tunnel collapsed. Then Ian watched Hannie tiptoe around to Leslie's fort and steal the snowballs hidden there.

Nobody looked as if he were having fun.

"You wrecked our fort!" Bobby yelled at Tammy. "I'm telling!"

"Liar! You are not going to tell!" Tammy shouted back. (Ian knew that was true.)

"Meanie!" Karen yelled at Chris. "Now *we* are going to destroy *your* fort. You just wait. You will see what we will do. We are going to win the snow war!"

"Thief!" Leslie yelled at Hannie. "You will be in big trouble for stealing, you know. Ms. Colman would not like it!"

She certainly would not, thought Ian. He opened his book. But Ms. Colman did not know what was going on. She did not know about the snow war. She was not on playground duty that month.

Ian wished once again that he could hurtle through space. He would hurtle far,

far away from the playground and the snow war.

That afternoon Ms. Colman told her students they could make snowflakes for half an hour. They had been making them in the afternoons and keeping them in their desks. Ian had made seven, and he was proud of them. He took them out of his desk and counted them.

Next to him Sara was doing the same thing. "One, two, three, four — hey, only *four*? I *know* I made six." She turned and looked at Terri. "*You* took them," she whispered.

"Did not."

In front of Ian, Tammy was muttering, "Hank, you give me back my scissors. They are my *own* scissors."

"I did not take them," Hank replied. (Ian saw that Hank was smiling.)

"Class," said Ms. Colman loudly, "I do not know what is going on here, but I would like you to get to work. If anyone sees Tammy's scissors, please return them.

In this class we do not take things that belong to other people. At least, not without asking first. Understand?"

The kids nodded.

And Ian thought, *I* know what is going on here. It is called a snow war. And I do not like it.

THE SNOWFLAKE WAR

Over the weekend Ian had plenty of time to read *They Came from Beyond*. He read and read. He read until the X-ers reached the fourth planet from their sun. By Sunday night, only three chapters were left in the book. Ian was excited. As soon as he finished *They Came from Beyond*, he was going to start the next book about the X-ers. It was called *Beyond Space*.

Beyond space, Ian thought. Hmm. Now that is funny. What could be beyond space except more space?

On Monday, Ian put both *They Came*

from Beyond and *Beyond Space* in his back-pack. Just in case. Just in case he read so much at recess that he finished the first book before the bell rang. He wanted to be able to start the second book right away.

Ian hurried into room 2A that morning. He hung up his jacket and ran to his desk. He could read for ten minutes before school started.

"Hey, Brain!" Bobby greeted him.

Ian did not even have a chance to answer. Before he could say hey back, he heard, "Oh, no! Oh, *no!*" from behind him.

Ian turned around. He saw Nancy, Hannie, and Karen peering into their desks.

"Four of mine are gone!" Nancy cried.

"Three of mine are gone," said Hannie.

"Well, *all* of mine are gone!" exclaimed Karen.

"All of your what?" asked Ian.

"My snowflakes," said Karen. "And I know who took them."

"Who?"

Karen glared across the room at Jannie. *"She* did."

Jannie glared right back at Karen. "Well, you wrecked part of our fort. And anyway, someone stole two of *my* snowflakes. And *I* know who did *that*." Now Jannie was glaring at Ricky.

"You guys — I mean, you *girls* — you broke down the back door to our fort," said Ricky. "Which means you are probably the ones who did *this*." Ricky held up a handful of torn snowflakes.

Oh brother, thought Ian.

"Class? What is going on here?"

Ian looked up. Ms. Colman was standing in the doorway. "I could hear you halfway down the hall," she said. "Ricky, what happened to your snowflakes?" Ms. Colman was frowning. She did not look happy.

"Jannie ripped them up," said Ricky.

"I did not!" cried Jannie. "But Ms. Colman, Ricky *took* two of my snowflakes. I

had five on Friday, and now I only have three."

"Jannie took all my snowflakes!" exclaimed Karen.

"Omar stole four of mine," said Terri.

"Did not!"

"Boys and girls," said Ms. Colman sharply. "Please sit down. I want absolute silence in this room."

The kids in Ms. Colman's class took their seats. No one said a word.

"Please place all of your snowflakes on your desks," said Ms. Colman.

Ian pulled out ten perfect snowflakes. Around him, his friends pulled out a few each. Some of them were torn.

Ms. Colman stared at them. "Why are you taking each other's snowflakes?" she asked quietly.

Nobody said a word. Ms. Colman waited for nearly a minute. At last she said, "This must stop. I am surprised that I have to say this to you, but you *must* leave each other's snowflakes alone. If you keep taking them, or ruining them, we will not have any for our booth, and then we will not be able to have a booth at the carnival."

Ms. Colman looked around the room. "I do not expect to have to say another word about this to you. Now clean off your desks. It is time to start the morning."

IAN'S TOOTH

That morning Ian's stomach felt funny. It did not exactly hurt. And he did not think his breakfast had disagreed with him. He just felt . . . nervous. That was it. Ian felt nervous. He decided he had butterflies in his stomach. And he decided he knew why. It was because Ms. Colman was cross with the class. Ms. Colman hardly ever got cross. And she almost never lost her temper. But Ian knew she was mad now. And he felt bad — even though he had nothing to do with the snow war or the snowflakes. None of his snowflakes was missing, and he had not taken anybody's.

All that morning, while Ian felt bad, his classmates were very quiet. Maybe they felt bad, too. Maybe they would even stop the snow war. Ian hoped so. And by lunchtime he felt better. That was because his classmates were behaving themselves. They did not say mean things to each other. They did not take things out of each other's desks. And they certainly did not steal any snowflakes. These were very good signs, thought Ian.

After lunch Ian ran outside with *They Came from Beyond* and *Beyond Space* stuffed into a big pocket in his jacket. He ran straight to his tree, and he sat on the rock. He looked out over the playground. And he saw his classmates gathering at their forts again.

"Oh, no," said Ian with a groan.

"Get out of here! Get out of my way!" Ian heard Audrey yell.

"No, you *girls* get away from *our* fort!" Bobby yelled back.

"You do not own this playground!" cried Karen.

Terri threw the first snowball. Hank threw the second. And Audrey threw the third. She threw it very hard. She was aiming at Ricky. But she missed. The snowball sailed across the playground. And it hit . . .

. . . Ian.

It hit him in the face.

"Ow, *ow*, OW!" shrieked Ian. The snowball had hurt. It had hurt much more than a snowball should hurt. Ian looked down. He saw blood in the snow. He touched his cheek. He saw blood on his mitten. *"Help!"* he cried.

"Brain, are you okay?"

Chris and Bobby ran to him.

"Brain? Ian?"

"I think my loose tooth came out," mumbled Ian.

The other kids gathered around Ian.

"Audrey, what did you throw?" asked Omar.

"Well . . . it was a sort of an iceball,"
admitted Audrey.

"An *ice*ball?" said a grown-up voice.
The voice belonged to Mr. Tang. He was
the teacher on playground duty. "All right.
Let's straighten things out here," he said.

Half an hour later the kids were in
their classroom again. Ian had been to the
nurse. He was still dabbing a wet paper
towel on the hole where his tooth had
been.

The classroom was silent. The kids were listening to Ms. Colman.

"I am glad you told Mr. Tang about the snow war," she said. (She certainly does not *look* glad, thought Ian.) "But I am not pleased with you. You let the snow war get out of hand. You brought it inside to our classroom. And Ian could have been hurt very badly. He is lucky that he only lost a tooth. So now I must tell you something. If the snow war does not stop right now, and if it does not stop completely, then we will not have our booth, and none of you may go to the carnival at all."

IAN GETS MAD

Ian could not believe his ears. His classmates could not believe theirs, either.

"Not *go* to the winter carnival?" repeated Nancy.

"That is what I said," replied Ms. Colman. "And I meant it."

If Ian's class had been quiet that morning, they were even quieter that afternoon. Everyone was quiet. Even Ms. Colman.

Ian knew the kids were embarrassed. No class had ever been told they could not go to the carnival.

Toward the end of the day Omar raised his hand. "But we can go to the car-

nival if the snow war stops, can't we?" he
said.

"Yes," agreed Ms. Colman. "But I am
going to be watching you carefully. So is
Mr. Tang."

Ian felt himself blush. He glanced
around the room. Some of his classmates
were looking at their hands. Some were
looking at the floor. Nobody was looking
at Ms. Colman — or at anyone else.

When the last bell rang that afternoon,

the kids jumped up from their desks. They hurried to their cubbies.

"This is all *your* fault," Tammy hissed to Bobby. "You threw the very first snowball."

"Did not," Bobby hissed back.

"Do not let Ms. Colman hear you!" Hank whispered.

"I won't. And anyway, this is *your* fault, Hank," said Bobby.

"Why is it mine?"

"It was your stupid idea to build a fort."

"Well, it was Ricky's idea to wreck the girls' forts."

"Was not!" exclaimed Ricky. "But it does not matter. Audrey was the one who threw the iceball."

"But Ian was the one sitting right out on a rock where anyone could hit him," whispered Audrey. She glared at Ian. "I guess the Brain is not so smart after all."

Ian opened his mouth. He was about

to yell at Audrey. He was about to point out that the rock was under a *tree,* for heaven's sake. Then he turned around and looked at Ms. Colman. She was sitting at her desk. And she was watching her students carefully. So Ian stuck his tongue out at Audrey. But he did not say a word to her. Then he stuck his tongue out at Ricky. And at Tammy. And at Bobby and Hank and even Chris. Then he marched out of the classroom.

Ian was mad. He was mad at every kid in the class. If the kids had not started the snow war, then they would not be in trouble. Ian was especially mad at Audrey. Who was so stupid she would throw an *ice*ball at someone? Audrey, that was who. Stupid, stupid, stupid. Ian was even mad at Ms. Colman. Ms. Colman had no right to say that *Ian* could not go to the carnival if the snow war did not stop. Ian had never been part of the snow war.

Ian was in a very bad mood when he woke up the next morning. He was still in a bad mood when he arrived at school. So he was particularly cross when he heard Mrs. Titus, the school principal, make this announcement over the loudspeaker: "Good morning, girls and boys. It has come to my attention that some of you have been holding snowball wars on the playground. Yesterday one of our students was injured when he was struck in the face by a snowball."

"It was an iceball," muttered Ian.

"So from now on, " Mrs. Titus continued, "there will be *no* snowball throwing on school property. At all. Ever."

Ian saw Audrey blush. Everyone in school would know that this was the fault of the kids in Ms. Colman's class.

"Aw, *man*," whispered Omar. "We cannot even throw snowballs anymore."

The other kids grumbled and muttered.

Karen said, "*Now* what are we going
to do at recess?"

And Ian replied, "I do not know, but
none of this is *my* fault."

12

THE SPACEMAN

All that morning in school Ian worked very hard. He paid attention to Ms. Colman. He kept his eyes on her or on his work. He did not look around at the other kids. He did not even look across the room at Chris.

When he heard Tammy complain that she was going to be sooooo booooored on the playground if she could not throw snowballs, he just stared down at his spelling words. When he saw Bobby making monkey faces at Natalie during silent reading, he just kept on reading.

At lunchtime Ian watched his classmates. Since they were all so mad at each other, he wondered where they would sit. They sat down at three tables in their three groups. But the groups did not seem very happy. Nobody was saying much. At Karen's table the girls did not even sit next to each other. They left empty chairs between their places.

"Rats and toads," said Ian.

Ian carried his lunch to an empty table. He sat down by himself.

"There is the Brain," said a voice from another table.

Ian stood up. He moved to a different chair. He sat down with his back to his classmates. Then he opened *Beyond Space* and began to read. He was in Chapter Four of his new book.

Once again the X-ers were hurtling through space. Only this time they wanted to hurtle to whatever was beyond space. Ian chewed and read, and read and chewed. He took a bite of his sandwich. And he tried once more to imagine himself hurtling through space.

Then — suddenly — Ian got a great, big, enormous, wonderful idea. It was so great that it made him forget about his classmates and their fight and the snow war. It nearly made him forget the X-ers. Ian jumped up. He stuffed his book in the pocket of his jacket and snapped the pocket shut. Then he tossed his trash in a garbage can. And then he found Mr. Morton, the cafeteria monitor.

"Mr. Morton? Could I take a tray with me to the playground today?" he asked. "Please?"

"What for?" asked Mr. Morton. Ian told him his great idea, and Mr. Morton said, "Well, I don't see why not. Go ahead."

So Ian zipped up his jacket, put on his hat and mittens, grabbed a cafeteria tray, and ran outside. He carried his tray to the top of the hill at the far end of the playground. Then he looked out at the rest of the playground. He saw his classmates trickling outside. Most of them stood around glumly. They looked sadly at their snowforts. Then they looked angrily at each other.

Well, thought Ian, *I* am not going to be all mad and bored and waste *my* recess.

Ian placed the tray in the snow at the top of the hill. He looked at the bottom of the hill. He thought of the X-ers hurtling through space. And then he knelt down, threw himself on the tray, pushed off with his feet, and . . . *whoosh!*

Ian was hurtling through space. He felt like an X-er.

He flew down the snowy hill on his stomach. The wind blew his hair back, and Ian could feel icy air on his cheeks.

At the bottom of the hill, the tray came to a gentle stop.

Yes! thought Ian.

Ian carried the tray back to the top of the hill. This time he sat on the tray and sailed down the hill on his bottom.

Hurtling through space, thought Ian.

Now I know why the X-ers like space travel so much.

At the bottom of the hill, Ian found himself looking up at Chris and Omar. Their eyes were shining.

"Cool idea, Ian," said Chris. "Can we try that?"

APOLOGIES

Ian, Omar, and Chris took turns flying down the hill on the tray.

"Hey, Brain! Was that your idea?" Ricky asked. He joined the boys at the bottom of the hill.

"It was *Ian's* idea," replied Chris.

"Oh, well . . . can I try it?"

"Maybe we should get another tray," said Omar.

"Get two more. We want to try, too," said Nancy.

The Three Musketeers had joined the boys. A bunch of the other girls were watching nearby.

In the end Mr. Morton gave the kids

in Ms. Colman's class six more trays. The kids spent the rest of recess flying down the hill. When the bell rang, they stacked the trays by the door to the cafeteria. Then they lined up to go inside.

"Ian?" said Audrey while they were waiting. "I am *really* sorry I threw that iceball at you. I did not mean to hit you, you know."

"I know," said Ian.

"And I should not have thrown it anyway. It could have hurt Ricky or whoever

it hit. But I did not think about that. I was too mad."

"It is okay," said Ian. "My tooth was going to come out soon anyway. And the Tooth Fairy gave me *double*, since it was knocked out. I got *two* dollars. Now I have almost enough to buy another book about the X-ers. They are my favorite books."

"Hannie," said Terri, "I am sorry I threw a snowball at you. I threw the first one yesterday. So . . . sorry."

"It is okay," replied Hannie.

Leslie tapped Bobby on the shoulder. "I am sorry I smashed in the side of your fort," she said.

Ian began to feel better. He was grinning. So was Audrey. So were Hannie and Terri and Leslie and Bobby. By the time the kids returned to their classroom, they were all smiling.

Ms. Colman smiled back at them. "Well," she said. "What is going on here? You look awfully happy."

"Ian had a good idea," Sara told her. "We went sledding on trays on the playground today."

"Ms. Colman?" said Audrey. "I told Ian I was sorry I threw the iceball at him. And I am sorry. Ian was not part of the snow war."

"No," said Leslie. "We got mad at Ian, but nothing was his fault."

"You know what?" spoke up Karen. "I did not really want to be so mad at everyone, especially not over the silly forts. So I should say I am sorry to Bobby and Ricky and Omar and Hank and Chris and Leslie and Audrey and Tammy and Terri and Jannie."

"We were not just mad at the other groups," added Ricky. "After yesterday we were all mad at each other."

"And at you, Ms. Colman," said Natalie. "We are sorry."

"I accept your apology," said Ms. Colman.

Ian sat at his desk and waited. He was waiting to hear Ms. Colman say the thing he thought she should say. When she did not say it, Ian raised his hand. "Ms. Colman," he began, "I think something is not fair. I think it is not fair that you told the *whole* class we could not go to the carnival if the snow war did not stop. Because *I* was not part of the snow war. Plus, I got hurt."

"Ian, you are right," agreed Ms. Colman. "That was not fair. I was not thinking. I guess I got as mad as the rest of you did. I am very, very sorry." She paused.

Then she smiled again and said, "I do not think we have to worry about the carnival anymore, though, do we? Is the snow war over?"

"*Yes!*" cried the kids in Ms. Colman's class.

SNIP, SNIP, SNIP

Now that the snow war was over, the kids in Ms. Colman's class could think about their snowflake booth again. And they had a lot of work to do.

"We need to build the booth," said Ms. Colman. "Maybe some of your parents could do that. Then we will paint it. We have to finish our snowflakes, of course. Also, we must think up fortunes to write on them. And we need to go shopping for the prizes."

Karen raised her hand. "My stepfather is a carpenter," she announced. "I bet he would help build the booth."

Ms. Colman called some of the parents

after school. Four of them decided to help Karen's stepfather build the booth in his workshop one Saturday. Meanwhile, in school, the kids worked on the snowflakes.

"We have only two weeks until the carnival," said Ms. Colman one morning. "I think that for part of every day we should divide into two groups. Half of you will cut out snowflakes. I will help the rest of you think of fortunes and write them on the snowflakes. How does that sound?"

"But I want to make snowflakes *and*

write fortunes!" cried Tammy. "Not just one or the other."

"Then the groups can switch," Ms. Colman replied.

On the first day Ian was part of the group writing fortunes. He and seven other kids joined Ms. Colman in the back of the room.

"I do not know what to write," said Natalie. "How do I know what is going to happen to people? How can I tell their fortunes?"

"Natalie, we are not *really* telling fortunes. Are we, Ms. Colman?" said Karen. "We will just make things up."

"The fortunes could be silly," added Omar.

"Like 'Be careful or you might kiss a frog today,' " said Leslie.

The kids giggled.

"How about 'Do not bend over when you are wearing a dress or people will see your underwear'?" suggested Audrey.

"Not *too* silly," said Ms. Colman. But she was smiling. "Also, remember that we have to be able to write the fortunes on the snowflakes, and there is not a lot of room. So keep the fortunes short."

"I know," said Ian. "How about 'Smile, and someone will smile back at you.' How is that?"

"Perfect," said Ms. Colman.

So the kids wrote fortune after fortune. And they snip, snip, snipped away at their snowflakes. Ms. Colman collected the new snowflakes in a box on her desk every day. The box was big. And it was getting full.

One day Ms. Colman said, "Class, we must shop for the prizes soon. We do not all need to go to the store. But five or six of you could come with me. We will go tomorrow after school. Sara's mother has agreed to come along and help out. Anyone who is interested in shopping tomorrow, talk to your parents tonight to see if you may go."

The next afternoon Ms. Colman, Ms. Ford, Sara, Ian, Nancy, Ricky, and Audrey went to the toy store in Stoneybrook. Ms. Colman brought along forty dollars. When they arrived, she said, "Remember — ten prizes, four dollars each. Okay, let's see what we can find."

The kids found so many great prizes that they had trouble choosing ten. They found art supplies and games and outdoor toys. They found some small stuffed animals and some dolls and trucks. At last Ms. Colman said, "Okay, kids. Just five more minutes to choose."

So they had to choose.

That weekend the parents built the booth. On Sunday the kids painted it. They were almost ready for the winter carnival.

THE WINTER
CARNIVAL

The winter carnival was to be held on Saturday. On Friday afternoon the students at Stoneybrook Academy set up their booths in the gym. When the kids in Ms. Colman's class peered into the gym, Sara gasped.

"It is so crowded!" she exclaimed.

And it was. Kids and teachers were everywhere. They were hammering and taping and cutting. They were taking things out of boxes. They were putting things on the walls. They were coloring in signs and setting out prizes.

"Our booth is back here," said Ms. Colman. "Karen's stepfather drove it here this morning."

The kids looked proudly at their booth. They had painted it bright blue. Then they had painted huge snowflakes on the background.

Now they got busy tacking snowflakes to all the walls inside their booth. They tacked them up so that the fortunes did not show. Then they displayed the ten prizes on a table in the booth. And finally they hung up their sign. The sign on the front of the booth read:

BUY A SNOWFLAKE!
JUST 50 CENTS!
READ YOUR FORTUNE OR
WIN A PRIZE!

Ian grinned. He thought the snowflake booth was the best one at the carnival. He could not wait until the next day.

When Ian and his parents and Chip

arrived at the carnival on Saturday morning, Ian could not believe his eyes. Overnight the teachers had changed the gym into a winter wonderland. Big snowflakes and snowballs hung from the ceiling. Along the walls were murals with snow scenes. And the mess from the day before was gone. In its place were all the booths, tidy and ready for the day. Two tables full of refreshments had been set up. At other booths things were for sale — crafts, and secondhand toys and clothes.

"Cool," said Chip. Ian could tell he was impressed.

"I have to work at our booth first," said Ian proudly. "For an hour. Then I get to walk around and play games and stuff."

"We will meet you at your booth in an hour then," said Mr. Johnson.

Ian joined Ms. Colman and Chris at the snowflake booth. The gym was starting to fill up. People wandered around. Kids decided which games they wanted to play.

The first person to buy a snowflake

was Mrs. Titus, the principal. Her snowflake had a fortune. The fortune read, "All your dreams will come true."

"How lovely," said Mrs. Titus.

The first person to win a prize was a girl from Mr. Posner's kindergarten class. She turned her snowflake over, and she sounded out the word *prize.* "Prize!" she shrieked. "I won a prize!" She chose a truck that could flip over if it bumped into a wall. "Thank you! Thank you! Thank you!" she said. "This is the best prize I ever won. I have never won a prize before."

When the hour was over, Ian's family met him and Chris. They walked around the carnival together. Ian played the ring toss and won a windup gorilla. (Chris won a mini Frisbee.) They each bought a baseball cap at the used-clothing table for just ten cents apiece.

Then Chip said, "Try the brownies. They are excellent." So Ian and Chris each bought a brownie.

Finally it was time to go home. After the Johnsons dropped Chris off at his house, Chip pulled something out of his pocket. He handed it to Ian. "I bought this at a secondhand booth for you," he said.

Ian looked at it. It was the next book about the X-ers. "For me?" he said. "Thanks!"

"Sure," said Chip.

Ian and Chip grinned at each other.

Ian could not wait to get home so he could start his new book.

L. GODWIN

About the Author

ANN M. MARTIN lives in New York and loves animals, especially cats. She has two cats of her own, Gussie and Woody.

Other books by Ann M. Martin that you might enjoy are *Rachel Parker, Kindergarten Show-Off* and the Baby-sitters Club series. She has also written the Baby-sitters Little Sister series starring Karen Brewer, one of the kids in Ms. Colman's class.

Ann grew up in Princeton, New Jersey, where she had many wonderful teachers like Ms. Colman. Ann likes ice cream, *I Love Lucy*, and especially sewing.

THE KIDS IN, MS. COLMAN'S CLASS

A new series by Ann M. Martin

Don't miss #6
TWIN TROUBLE

"Tammy, Tammy! I finished *two* and a *half* books this weekend! Isn't that great? That is a record for me! How many books did you read?" (Tammy had been reading all weekend too.)

"Well, um . . ." Tammy began. "Um, I read five and a half books." Tammy looked sorry. "I did not mean to. I was just reading along, and before I knew it . . ."

"That is okay," said Terri slowly. "You should not apologize. We are supposed to read as much as we can. The more we read, the more money our library will get."

"But still," said Tammy.

"I know," said Terri.

"What happened to us?" asked Tammy. "Why aren't we samesies?"

Meet some new friends!

THE KIDS IN MS. COLMAN'S CLASS

by Ann M. Martin

There's always something going on in Ms. Colman's class! Read about the adventures of Baby-sitters Little Sister® Karen Brewer...and everyone else in the second grade.

☐ BBZ26215-7 **The Kids in Ms. Colman's Class #1: Teacher's Pet** $2.99

☐ BBZ26216-5 **The Kids in Ms. Colman's Class #2: Author Day** $2.99

☐ BBZ69199-6 **The Kids in Ms. Colman's Class #3: Class Play** $2.99

☐ BBZ69200-3 **The Kids in Ms. Colman's Class #4: Second Grade Baby** $2.99

☐ BBZ69201-1 **The Kids in Ms. Colman's Class #5: The Snow War** $2.99

Scholastic Inc., P.O. Box 7502, 2931 East McCarty Street, Jefferson City, MO 65102

Please send me the books I have checked above. I am enclosing $_____ (please add $2.00 to cover shipping and handling). Send check or money order—no cash or C.O.D.s please.

Name_____Birthdate____/___/__

Address_____

City_____State/Zip_____

Please allow four to six weeks for delivery. Offer good in U.S. only. Sorry mail orders are not available to residents of Canada. Prices subject to change. KMC696